Love
ON A
Young Brunette

Love on a Young Brunette

CHUONG VAN NGUYEN

THE REGENCY
PUBLISHERS

Copyright © 2023 Chuong Van Nguyen.

All rights reserved. No part of this book may be reproduced in any form or by any electronic or mechanical means, including information storage and retrieval systems, without permission in writing from the author and publisher, except by reviewers, who may quote brief passages in a review.

ISBN: 978-1-960113-48-1   (Paperback Edition)
ISBN: 978-1-960113-49-8   (Hardcover Edition)
ISBN: 978-1-960113-47-4   (E-book Edition)

Some characters and events in this book are fictitious and products of the author's imagination. Any similarity to real persons, living or dead, is coincidental and not intended by the author.

Book Ordering Information

The Regency Publishers, International
7 Bell Yard London WO2A2JR

info@theregencypublishers.com
www.theregencypublishers.international
+44 20 8133 0466

Printed in the United States of America

Once upon a time there was a beautiful young girl with brunette hair name Shelly that just had finished and graduated from high school.

After her graduations and celebrations, she later moves on to university studying Medicines and medical sciences beginning of next year. After her graduation, her long period of holiday break was over. She was getting ready to start Uni the next following day.

The next morning, she went to the institute feeling nervous and all due to her first day. While her class is starting, she sits there paying attention to the teacher, she didn't know that there was a man walking pass by the classroom staring at her. It was the janitor, and his name is Nathan, in his mid-30's.

He couldn't keep an eye off her noticing just how beautiful she really is. Shelly turns her head thinking that there's someone might be looking at her in the hallway of the rear door. She only saw a glimpse of someone but not clearly because that somebody she didn't know had walked off before her eyes. She then turns back and pays attention to the teacher without caring any less about it.

The janitor Nathan walking slowly thinking to himself just how beautiful she really is. Thinking that would someone like her Caucasian with brunette hair be interest in someone like him which is Asian appearance.

Later that afternoon when he finishes end of his shift, he came home laying on his bed daydreaming about the girl he saw today in the morning. He is having some fetishes about her fantasizing having sex. He is masturbating her constantly all afternoon till evening. He finally stops when he is so saw and tired.

I've got the hots for you baby, he said!

He suddenly gotten so tired that he fell asleep afterwards.

The next following day he arrived to work with some roses he bought in the morning before heading to the institute. When he arrived there, he went to her classroom and ask the teacher there what her name was that is sitting on that specific table since yesterday that he is pointing at, and she told him that her name is Shelly!

He came and put the roses on her desk and thanks the teacher for telling him who she was. The class was not started yet. Everything was still too early. Not a single student has come yet. Nobody saw Nathan put the roses on her desk but except the teacher from Shelly's class. He then walks off back to his work with a smile on his face, hoping things will turn out to be like it sounds.

That morning, lots of students have come and Shelly showed up too. Shelly went into her classroom seeing some roses on her desk where she usually sits. She picks it up and smells them. The roses are beautiful, she says. Nathan is spying on her. He can see from his view that she looks kind of happy and grateful.

She doesn't know who's these roses belong to, she wonders?

Again, she thinks someone is spying on her at the hallway and she turns around to see who it is, and she sees someone for a glimpse again walking away fast! So, this time she goes out to the room and sees who it is walking pass by the hallway staring at her. And all she saw was a few students and a janitor, but she doesn't know that it was him who gave the rose to her yet. She then went back to her classroom sitting at her desk asking her classmate beside her does she know who's these roses belong to? She said to her she doesn't know either who they belong to.

She was very happy to receive a gift from someone anonymous but find it quite odd and anxious to know where or who it belongs to. After when the bell rang for the student's lunch break, she goes around to people asking if they know who gave her these roses to her. But none of them neither knows who it belongs to either until one person came up and told her who it belongs to. It was her teacher from her class. She told Shelly that those roses came from the Janitor and he's name is Nathan. While her teacher is talking to her, Nathan is around the corner standing there spying on them both listening to what they're talking about. And as to that moment, he does not like what he has heard from a short-range distance. He can hear her saying horrible things about him. She's saying these roses belong to that janitor! And the teacher said yes and that he likes you! Ewe, shelly said. These roses belong to that fat and ugly Janitor guy name Nathan. I do not want to date or have anything to do with a dude like him that cleans toilets and stuff.

She walks off and said thanks to the teacher for telling her who the roses belonged to. She went to the bin and threw them away.

Nathan is now heart broken, he's heart is pounding irregularly, and tears is running down he's eyes. He couldn't handle the rejection and is so hurt inside of himself. He now feels so miserable that day. He told the principal of the institute that he needs some time off, so he came up with an excuse. He was absent of his duties. The next day and days later Nathan can not be seen at the institute doing his duties and Shelly notices it too, but she did not care for less about him.

Around six months later, everything was like normal as usual, Shelly's course for the 1st semester was almost over.

Shelly is walking out of the classroom with her books held in her arms going to her locker until something has gotten to her eyes. She sees a new employee working as a janitor, a very good-looking handsome janitor. She couldn't keep her eyes off him which same goes to the rest of the other female students. She just keeps on staring at him wondering who he is until her class teacher came up to her and snap her out of it. Her teacher told her that she has forgotten one of her books back from the classroom and said to her does she know who that janitor guy is that she keeps on staring at. No, Shelly says.

She doesn't know who he is but thinks and says it's one of the new guys.

Wrong! Her teacher replies. That isn't the new janitor! That is Nathan! The same person that gave you the roses almost months ago and then rejected him.

Really Shelly says!

She remember that he was overweight and now couldn't believe just how much weight he has now loss and changed since then.

Her teacher explained to her that Nathan needed some time off due to his depression that he was going through and needed to cut back on his size. He is now 81kg and use to weigh 120kg. Big change she says.

Her teacher continues to ask her does she like him now? Shelly's reply was kind of! He just looks so beautiful now, she said.

Her teacher tells her to go introduce herself to him before someone else does. After Shelly is walking to him, her teacher walks off back to minding her business. While Shelly is walking towards him, she can see him doing something with his cleaning trolley. She's feeling so nervous to be coming to him after she notice herself that she rejected his roses a while back.

She finally came up to him but doesn't know what to say at first. The only words she could think of is Hi there! So, she said it. Nathan looks right at her and said hi back in a nice soft voice.

Um were you the one who gave me the roses beginning of this year, she asks! Yes, he replied!

Why did you give me the rose may I ask?

Because I think you're pretty that's why I gave you the rose, he said. You're too, she replies.

They both took it as a compliment.

Nathan was thinking to himself at that very moment the day how she reacted by throwing the roses in the bin and called him fat and ugly. Since he has now slim down that is the time where she comes. The rejection from her has made him change his appearance, but anyhow he shook her hand and introduce himself to her and same goes to her and she told him she already knows who he is basically from her teacher.

They were about to go on their separate ways until she asks him does he want to go on a date with her since he tried to give her the roses.

He accepted and she smiled back at him. They exchanged phone numbers. While they were doing that, Shelly asks him does he want to go to the amusement park this weekend with her. Sure thing, he said.

They then went home in their separate ways.

The next day in the morning, Shelly gets a call from Nathan asking her if she would like to hang out to the park to have a picnic with him before heading to the amusement park later this evening.

She accepted and went later. When she arrived there to see him at the park, she hugged him. They both then went and sat on the bench together and enjoyed their picnic. They were eating, drinking and talking a lot. After when they finished up, moments later they went and lay on the grass of the oval looking up in the sky seeing clouds and blue sky shinning with sunlight on them. while both are laying there, Shelly compliments on the weather saying just how beautiful it really is. She later puts her right arm around him also complimenting on him saying that he looks so hot like a movie star.

They both gotten so drowsy due to the food they ate and all that talking for a few hours, they taken a nap there for awhile like a baby.

A few hours have pass by, they woken up and getting ready to go and head to the amusement park for even more fun and enjoyment.

Took them one and a half hour to get there. When they had finally arrived, they both are very excited and can't wait to go on the rides and play some games. Shelly grabs Nathan's wrist and dragged him to one of the game sections. Hours of fun time, Shelly needed to go to the toilet, and she went while Nathan is in the other hand busy waiting in line to buy some food. When she's done, she heads out to see Nathan and noticing him standing with two other girls laughing and smiling at each other. One of the girls then kisses him on the side of his cheeks.

Shelly wasn't too happy to what she has seen, she is very angry to be seeing someone kissing her boyfriend like that. So, she walks away in a hurry and leaves him there at the amusement park. Nathan sees her leaving and tells her to wait and told the girls that he had to go now. He saw her face and knew she's not too happy about it. He knows she thinks that the two girls are trying to pick him up because of his good looks but that's not what it seems, and he wants to tell her that, but he suddenly lost her in the crowd and couldn't find her anywhere.

Moments of searching for her, he couldn't tell where she had gone to, and he started to panic. He then tries to call her on her mobile but there was no answer!

He stayed around the amusement park for a while until its almost closed. He stayed to see if she would re-appear but unfortunately the fun park has now been closed. She has left and went home some time ago where he does not know when.

He too went home after that. When he came home, he lay on his bed feeling exhausted. Afterwards he gave a one last time on calling her, and she finally answers his call, but he wasn't happy of what she said. She told him to go away and then hangs up!

He knew she was upset and was going to say something like that.

The next following day, he got refresh from yesterday.

Afterwards, he tried reach to out and call Shelly again. She picks up the phone, answers him saying that she hates him and does not want to see him ever again. (Hangs up the phone)

He never got the chance to say a single word and she hangs up the phone. He calls her again, but she did not answer back so he started texting instead. He is writing to her telling just how very sorry he is, and its not like what it seems. He explains to her in text the whole situation, that the two girls that kiss him are from university. The same institute that she goes to. They were all friends there, and the kiss was just from the side cheeks not the lip, he wrote.

Since he texts her that, he did not see a reply text back at that moment. Then hours and days. He might as think she truly had given up on him. He didn't give up on her yet, but he gave it a rest. He was about to give it about a week to see if she would call him back, but if she does not then he will let her go!

A week later the time was over, and he said to himself (I guess she's not going to call me) so he decided to have gone on their separate ways. Just by luck at that split second, she calls him, and he was surprised. He didn't think she would ever call him back, and he thought it was over between them.

She asks him if they could meet up at the park, that they met up a week ago.

Are you alright, he asks!

So, are we back together again?

She was quiet for a second, and then she said to him "just meet her at the park." (Hangs up the phone).

Later, he arrives at the park where she asks him to come. He sees her standing there waiting for him. While approaching her, he doesn't know if she is whether still upset about the other time of the incident or if she had moved on.

When he got up to her, he asks is she still upset with him on the other day. She didn't say anything at first but just gave him a hug instead!

He was surprised why she did that. She said to him that she is very sorry. Sorry for being a hot-tempered girl. She told him that she couldn't help herself for being jealous, and took it the wrong way.

This is just all a misunderstanding, Nathan says.

Understood, said she.

They both are now back together again. They walked and talked with a happy smile on their faces for a while at the oval of the park. They both left after that. A few days have passed by, they both went to the theatres to watch a movie. They enjoyed watching until Nathan wanted to go buy a bag of popcorn. Shelly tells him to buy extra bag for her too along the way.

When he went and bought the two bags of popcorn, he hid one of them behind him to make it look like he only purchases one, to make a joke on her to see her reaction. When he got in the cinema room and sat next to her, he pulled that little joke and things didn't turn out like what he expected to be. She only sees one bag of popcorn that he is holding but not two and he is eating on his own. Where's her one, she asks! Bought only one for me, he said. You're such a tight ass, she said!

She got upset and left the cinema room. He told her to wait; all this was just a joke! But she just stubbornly neglected him. He tried to show her the extra popcorn bag that he purchases in front of her while chasing after her. She didn't care for less and grabs the bag threw it at him. The popcorn was all over him and onto the floor.

She continued getting away from him. He stands there yelling at her saying why do you always take things so seriously!

They went home in their separate ways and end up not finishing watching the movie.

Nathan got back to his home walking back and forward in his room feeling very angry to as why something small causes a major issue!

He then tries to ring her, but she doesn't pick up. So, he calls her repeatedly until she answers back. She told him to stop calling her, you tight ass! And hangs up the phone. Again, he never got the chance to say a single word back. So, he began texting her. While he was doing that, she suddenly calls him. He stops texting and answers the phone. She said she's sorry.

Why is it that your always taking things so seriously, he asks!

She doesn't know why she is like that either. He began to say to her that he loves her so much and wants her to stop taking things seriously. I love you too, she says!

They both were talking to each other for a while, planning to meet up with each other at some place and Shelly decided it was at the creek. They agreed and plan to meet up tomorrow.

Afterwards when they had finish chatting, there was something very suspicious going on with Shelly. She is up to something, but Nathan doesn't know it.

Plan jokes on me! "saying to herself" then I make jokes on you to see if you can handle it. Love me, then I put that to a test also.

The next following day she and Nathan met up together at her house. They met and hugged each other like as if nothing had ever happened since yesterday's issue.

Shelly borrows her family's car to get to the creek. And off they went. She had driven for a while and when they have arrived there, she stayed in the car and told Nathan to get out and help her unpack all the stuff first for another picnic. While he was unpacking, he asks her isn't she coming out to have some fresh air. Her response was no, she said to him she prefers to stay in the car for a while rather then being outside. So, he continued unpacking. When he was doing that, Shelly turned on the ignition of the car and sped off. She can be seen laughing while driving.

Jokes on me huh, how about jokes on you, she said!

Nathan turns around and sees her driving off. He is chasing after her telling her to wait but she sped off too quick. He was trying to tell her to wait and come back but apparently, she couldn't hear him from a far range. He suddenly stops chasing after her. He stood there feeling very upset.

He then walks back home leaving all the stuff behind. He wanted to call her, but he left his phone in her car. He kept on walking hoping that she would turn around back to get him but unfortunately, she never came back. He is very hurt inside of himself to as why she would be doing something like this. He doesn't know for sure why she left him deserted. He is guessing that it might be from yesterday.

While walking he couldn't believe something petty like yesterdays incident would make a person get so upset like that. Such a sensitive chick, he says!

Hours of long walking, he finally made it back, but he didn't go back to his house but made it to Shelly's. when he gotten there, he was standing at her lawn looking at her window from the outside front of her yard. She can be heard talking and laughing on the phone to her friend.

He hears her and gets very furious yelling out at her. She hears him and covers her mouth for a second. She then hangs up the phone.

Oh, my he's back, she said!

She came to the window from her room looking down and sees Nathan standing there looking upset.

He continued to yell at her saying "why did you leave me there at the creek and drive off, is it because of the joke that I've made yesterday."

Yes, she replies!

She told him that it was just a joke and that she was only playing around like he did.

That is no joke, he said!

He explained to her that he's joke was just small and that she has a sensitive personality. And that she's very easy to get mad at things.

She laughs at him and said she is sorry.

That is not funny, he says!

She sticks her head back inside and went down to see him. When she does, she asks him is he still mad at her?

He did not say anything to her but just gave her the upset look like she knows he is still mad. She said that she will never leave him like that ever again.

Do you still love me, she asks?

Yes, he replied!

They both hugged each other. While she was hugging him, she is speaking in her mind saying that this is not over yet, and giggles!

That night she drove him back home. When he arrived home, she gave him a kiss. He then went inside his apartment and slept like a baby. Tired of all that long walking.

The next day in the afternoon, Shelly calls Nathan on the phone asking him if he would like to come and have dinner with her family at her place.

Most definitely, he said!

She told him not to be late.

Later that evening he arrived at her house and wasn't so pleasant surprise at all. He sees everybody is already enjoying and eating their dinner without him. And again, he felt outraged. He felt left out. He came up to Shelly and tells her off in a small tone voice, why is that everybody almost finish eating their meal without him. Is this another one of your tricks, he said!

She said to him no, in a lying way but she knows she did It on purpose again to hurt his feelings. She wanted to test him out to see how far he will go.

She told him that he was not supposed to be late and that everyone couldn't wait anymore, so they had to go ahead and eat without him.

Late, he said! I was only a "few minutes late!"

She is sorry and told him next time to come a bit earlier as possible.

He gave her the stare for a moment and gave a deep breath.

Ok, he said!

Shelly turns around walks off smiling in a way knowing that she has got him again and got away with it. Nathan then went home on that day. When he arrived home, straight away he got a call from

Shelly. She asks him if he would like to go on a skiing trip with her to the snowy mountains tomorrow.

Sounds great, he says!

But there's not going to be any dirty tricks, he said!

No, she replies!

He accepts. The next following day during the morning, they have arrived at the place. When they arrived, they had so much fun skiing and playing around with the snow. While they were playing, Shelly was about to pull another joke on him again until he accidentally did something to her first. When he was playing with the snow, he rolled up the snow making it into a ball, he also accidentally picks up a small rock with it without him knowing and rolling it together and throws it at her. He was supposed to throw it at her body not her face and that's where the problem became a major issue. Things didn't turn out as it expected for him.

Shelly can be heard screaming and crying in pain. Blood can be seen running down from her mouth.

"You asshole, she said!"

He is very sorry, he said. He told her he didn't know that there was a solid object inside the snowball. And he was supposed to throw it at the body not the face!

He came up to her trying to calm her down and help her, but she didn't want his help and pushed him away.

She left that scene and went to the hospital by herself, leaving Nathan behind. Moments later when she arrived at the hospital, the nurses tried to fix up her swollen mouth. The doctors told her to stay here for the whole night. They say she will be fine by tomorrow morning and will get discharged by then. She let her family know that she's in the hospital and that she is doing ok and be leaving the facility by tomorrow.

The next day in the morning she got discharged and went home.

When she came back home, she wasn't so pleasantly surprised. She didn't expect to see Nathan there inside her house talking to her parents.

Her parents tell her that Nathan is here to see her and and that he has explain everything and the whole situation. He is very sorry to see what has happen and that it was an accident!

She just ignored them all and continuing walking up stairs into her room. She then slams the door!

Her parents told Nathan to go up stairs and try to talk to her. He listens to them and goes up and stands right at her door inhaling in a deep breath, ready to go in. he knocks on the door but no answer so he decided to let himself in. when he came in her room, he can see her sitting at her desk doing her studies. He comes right up to and beside her. She notices that he is standing there but act like she doesn't care.

Nathan then speaks, telling her just how sorry he is when he threw the snowball at her. He told her that he didn't know there was a small rock inside it and that it was supposed to hit the body not the face.

She continues to ignore him.

He then takes out his small expensive gift box and tries to show it at her face, but she didn't look. So, he continues to explain to her that this box contains a ring in it. It is an engagement ring!

"I want to marry you, he said!" love at first sight and I know it's only been a few weeks since we know each other. but I want to marry you!

So, he puts the engagement ring on her table next to her sitting.

She put the pen down and grabs the small box and throws it in the bin next to beside her and continues to write again.

He is so hurt to see her doing something like that in front of him. He has a one final brief to say to her, he tells her that he loves her so much and tried he's best to treat her with love and respect. Tears can be seen running down he's eyes while he is explaining to her.

He continues to tell her that he is very sorry for coming into her life in the first place, hurting her feelings and physically.

I love you, and I guess love hurts so much!

He then tries to feel her hair with his hand, but she didn't let him and whacks his hand away.

He couldn't take it anymore. He said to her a final goodbye, and he won't be seeing her again.

Take care, he said.

He walks off out of the house. She stops writing at that split second and hears him going down the stairs. She quickly goes up to her window and looks down at him. She sees him crying while going to his car. she then runs down the stairs out of her house crying also, feeling sorrowful of what he said to her.

"Please don't go, come back, she said!"

She opens the front house door and chases after him, but he already driven away.

She keeps on saying I'm so sorry, please come back many times.

Her parents came out of the house and tells her off. They told her that she won't be seeing him again.

They saw the look on his face and that they know for certain that he does not want to see their daughter again. They all went back inside including Shelly. Shelly came up to her room and grabs the ring in the box from the bin she threw. She came to her bed opens the box and looks at the nice shiny expensive engagement ring that he given her. She said it is beautiful and lays down her bed crying even more. She now feels extremely guilty for the way how she treated him and was too stubborn to listen to him about the accident.

A few days of silent, university was about to start again for a new semester. The next following day, Shelly came to school walking pass by the hallways to see if Nathan was working there but unfortunately, she never did see him. When her class starts, during her period she is always turning her head to see if he is walking pass by or standing at her classroom door looking at her. But he's not there. Same goes with the next day and the day after that, and still no sign of him anywhere. She felt very sad that she no longer wants to study and walks out of the classroom.

She doesn't know where to find him, so she goes to the park where they use to hang out for the first time and goes there to chill out. When she has gotten to the park. She kept on looking down at the grass while sitting at the bench. She was sitting there for hours thinking about him hoping that he might showed up to see her. She misses him so much. She then tries to call him but he's number is invalid.

He deleted he's number and which made her even more sad and depressed. She's sitting there crying.

She did it again and again days and days going to the park sitting there waiting for him to might show but he never came. She now realized that he is never coming back to see her and that he's long gone. Her last resort was driving to his home. When she came there, there was no luck also. He had already left he's apartment.

During that day, she went back home into her room thinking about Nathan. She felt so sorrowful and depressed that she could no longer take it anymore. She was about to commit suicide by tying a rope around her neck and hanged herself, until her parents came in and saw it. They quickly stopped her from doing it. They tried to calm her down and stopping her from continuing. They finally calm her down, but they were too scared themselves, don't know what else to do but to call the police for help. Later, the police have arrived and their recommendation to her parents was her to be taken by them to the mental hospital to get treated.

The following hour she got transfer from police custody to the institute. The doctors talk to her, but she doesn't say anything back to them. So, they decided to keep her in the facility for a time being.

While she's been in there, the workers and the doctors notice she doesn't talk to anyone. She only sits around by herself looking down at the floor most of the time.

Wherever she does or what ever she goes, the only thing in her head is thinking about Nathan.

Every night in her room unit, she can be heard screaming in pain for Nathan. That's all she can think of is him. Every night the nurses always give her medication to calm herself down.

Three months later, she is finally rehabilitated and feeling so much better then ever. The doctors notice and assess her that she no longer has suicidal thoughts. So, they decided to discharge her on the day.

Her parents got a call from them and went to come pick her up. They finally came to get her, and Shelly was so happy to have seen her parents. They hugged each other and left the mental institute.

While driving all the way home, her mom asks her if she would like to go to the amusement park.

She told her "whatever" it's better then staying at the mental hospital for months without any enjoyment.

Even though she has got rehabilitated, she still feels sad inside, but trying to hide it from everyone.

Moments later, they have finally arrived at the amusement park. Her parents asked her is she happy to come here?

I guess so, she said!

While walking to each section of the games, she's always walking behind her mom and dad looking down feeling sad. She tries to be happy but couldn't as much. The three was then standing in line waiting for the food truck. Until something has gotten Shelly's eyes. She doesn't know for sure if what she sees is true from a far distance. She sees someone that looks exactly like Nathan crouching down giving two kids an ice cream cones.

She walks closer and closer to see if its really him. She yells out to him calling Nathan, Nathan!

He gets up and sees her. He sees her and wasn't happy, but she was. He then runs away from her.

"Come back, please come back, she says!"

She can be seen running and crying while chasing after him. She chases after him all the way to the bushes. He then hides himself behind the tree where Shelly could not see and find him. It was a dead end at that point and nowhere else to run.

Shelly also stopped at that point and is looking around to see where he is but couldn't find him anywhere. She knows he is hiding somewhere around the area.

She tries to talk to him out of this explaining to him that she is sorry, sorry for hurting him and that she misses him so much. She told him that she tried to commit suicide too and just got discharge today from the hospital.

Tears can be seen running down Nathan's eye by listening to what she has said. He understands but is being stubborn also due to the hurtful things she has done to him. So, he ignores her and runs away from her again. She sees him running off and she chases after him again also. She yelled out to him telling him to "wait, please come back!"

They kept on chasing each other until for that moment he accidentally trips on a tree branch and fell over to the ground. He tries to get back up quickly to get away from her until she runs up and hugs him so tightly from behind not letting him go.

He tried to pull both her arms off him, but she was holding on to his waist so tightly.

"Let go, he says!"

"Please, please, she said!" I love you so much. She is crying holding on to him.

He then manages to pull her both arms away and pushes her off him. She then gets back up and hugs him again on his chest, but he kept pushing her away and she kept on coming back up to him.

He told her to go away and that he doesn't love her anymore. But she kept on saying sorry to him all the time until he finally gave up and forgives her.

She tells him that she loves him so much and love also hurts so much just exactly like how he said it to her a while back.

"I know, he said."

"Kiss me, please kiss me she asks!"

He didn't kiss her yet, but she just went and did it to him anyways. She was the one that kiss him first.

They both hugged and kissed each other at that very moment. She asks him to marry her and that she still got his engagement ring.

She promises him also, to never have hurt him again like what she did. She said to him that she regrets it and has now learn her lesson.

Some time later they both got married, settle down and had kids. With the luck of jackpot that Nathan had won during the power ball game. He claimed millions in prize winning. Shelly no longer studies due to family and with the money that Nathan won, there was no need to work for some time. They carefully spent their fortune and lived happy ever after.

The End

www.ingramcontent.com/pod-product-compliance
Lightning Source LLC
LaVergne TN
LVHW040203080526
838202LV00042B/3299